Mrs. Barr Has Gone Too Far!

Dan Gutman

Pictures by
Jim Paillot

HARPER
An Imprint of HarperCollinsPublishers

Thanks to Katie Fishcher
and Reid Heicklen

My Weirder-est School #9: Mrs. Barr Has Gone Too Far!
Text copyright © 2021 by Dan Gutman
Illustrations copyright © 2021 by Jim Paillot
All rights reserved. Printed in the United States of America.

Library of Congress Control Number: 2021938241
ISBN 978-0-06-291079-0 (pbk bdg) — ISBN 978-0-06-291080-6 (lib. bdg)

Typography by Laura Mock
21 22 23 24 25 PC/LSCH 10 9 8 7 6 5 4 3 2 1
❖
First Edition

Contents

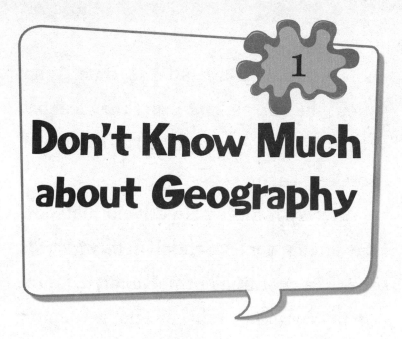

Don't Know Much about Geography

My name is A.J. and I know what you're thinking. You're thinking about the Great Lakes.

What makes the Great Lakes so great? That's what I want to know. If you ask me, lakes shouldn't brag. If they were *really* great, they wouldn't have to talk about how great they are all the time. What about the *other* lakes? Don't they feel bad because they're not great? Is there a Not-So-Great Lake?

Anyway, it was a perfectly normal Monday at Ella Mentry School. In other words, there was nothing normal about it. I hung up my coat in my cubby. That's when my teacher Mr. Cooper came flying into the room. He tripped over somebody's backpack and did a face-plant into the garbage can.

"I'm okay!" he said as he took the can off his head. Then we pledged the allegiance and did Word of the Day.

"Should we turn to page twenty-three

in our math books?" asked Andrea Young, this annoying girl with curly brown hair.

"No," said Mr. Cooper.

"Are we going to do silent reading?" asked Andrea's crybaby friend, Emily.

"No."

"Science?" asked Ryan, who will eat anything, even stuff that isn't food.

"No."

"Can we go home?" I asked. I figured it was worth a shot.

"No," replied Mr. Cooper. "Today, we're going to do something *different*."

Uh-oh. I didn't like the sound of that. Different is *scary*. You never know what's gonna happen. Different could be good, or it could be bad.

"What are we going to do?" asked Michael, who never ties his shoes.

"This morning," said Mr. Cooper, "we're going to see a slideshow."

Noooooooooooooooooo!

Not a slideshow! *Anything* but a slideshow! Slideshows are super boring. I'd rather jump into a volcano wearing a pink tutu than watch a slideshow.

"I'm going to show you pictures of my trip to Spain," said Mr. Cooper.

Nooooooooooooooooooo!

Mr. Cooper went to Spain to visit his sister. We had a sub for a week while he was gone.

He turned on his computer and plugged it into the smartboard.

"Oh, you're going to like this," he told us. "Spain was amazing. I was like a fish out of water."

Huh? What did fish have to do with anything?

"Here's me at the Royal Palace in Madrid," Mr. Cooper said when his first slide flashed on the screen.

"Ooooh, it's *beautiful*!" said Andrea, who thinks everything is beautiful.

I was already feeling drowsy. I felt my eyelids getting heavy.

"Here's my sister at a church in Barcelona," said Mr. Cooper.

I was fighting off sleep.

"Here's a man playing guitar outside the walled city of Toledo," he continued.

Zzzzzzzzz.

"Here's my sister at a fruit market."

What a snoozefest!

"Here's my sister at a bullfight," said Mr. Cooper.

"Bullfights are cool," said Neil, who we call the nude kid even though he wears clothes.

"I think bullfighting is cruel to animals," said Andrea. "I don't approve of violence."

"What do you have against violins?" I asked her.

"Not violins, Arlo! Violence!"

I was just yanking Andrea's chain. I know the difference between violins and violence.

Mr. Cooper's PowerPoint torture went on for a million hundred minutes. He went over to a big map on the wall.

"Who can find Spain on the map?" he asked.

Andrea waved her hand in the air like she had to go to the bathroom really badly.

"How about you, A.J.?" asked Mr. Cooper. "Can you point to Spain?"

I didn't know where Spain was. But I got up and went over to the map.

"Here?" I asked, pointing to some big area near the bottom.

"That's Antarctica," said Mr. Cooper.

"Here?" I asked.

"That's Greenland," said Mr. Cooper.

"Here?"

"That's Australia!"

Mr. Cooper rubbed his forehead.

"Oooooooohhhh!" groaned Andrea. "I know where Spain is!"

Mr. Cooper called on her. She went up and pointed to some area near the middle of the map.

"That's right!" said Mr. Cooper. "Very good, Andrea."

Andrea went back to her seat, smiling the smile that she smiles to let everybody know she knows something nobody else knows. Why can't a truck full of maps fall on Andrea's head?

"Okay," said Mr. Cooper. "Who can find China?"

Andrea was the only one with her hand

in the air. All the rest of us stared at the floor. If you don't know the answer to a question, stare at the floor so the teacher won't call on you. That's the first rule of being a kid.

"It's right *here!*" Mr. Cooper said, pointing at the map. "How about Turkey? Can anybody other than Andrea find Turkey?"

That's a ridorkulous question. Why would a turkey be on a map? Was somebody using the map as a dinner plate? We all stared at the floor.

"How about Greece?" asked Mr. Cooper. "Where's Greece?"

"Is it turkey grease?" asked Alexia, this

girl who rides a skateboard all the time.

"Somebody should clean that map off," I said. "It's making me Hungary."

Only a few kids laughed at my hilarious joke.

"How about Africa?" asked Mr. Cooper. "Surely, you can find *that*. It's a very large continent!"

I know what a continent is. That's when you poop your pants. But it would have been rude to say that out loud.

"I can point to Africa!" shouted the Human Homework Machine.

"How about you, Emily?" asked Mr. Cooper.

Emily looked nervous as she went over

to the map. She pointed at a continent.

"That's not Africa!" said Mr. Cooper. "That's South America!"

I thought Emily might cry. Mr. Cooper rubbed his forehead again.

"This is basic geography, you guys!" he said. "Can anybody find Russia? Germany? Finland?"

I raised my hand.

"Yes, A.J.?"

"I can't find them on the map," I said. "But if you're Russian to the bathroom, and you're German before you wash your hands, and you're Finnish when you leave, what are you while you're *in* the bathroom?"

"I give up," said Mr. Cooper. "What are you?"

"You're a-peein'!" I shouted. "Get it? You're a-peein'?"*

Mr. Cooper rubbed his forehead and mumbled something under his breath about early retirement.

---

* That is the greatest joke in the history of the world.

A Real Globetrotter

I thought that was the end of our geography lesson. But it wasn't! The next day, we were in the middle of silent reading, and guess who walked through the door.

Nobody! You can't walk through a door! Doors are made of wood.

But our principal, Mr. Klutz, walked through the door*way*. He has no hair at all. I mean *none*. He can probably wax his car and his head at the same time.

"Mr. Cooper told me you kids are having trouble with geography," said Mr. Klutz. "So I said he could bring in someone to help you learn about it. Mrs. Barr, will you come in, please?"

A lady came into the classroom. She had bracelets and necklaces dangling all over her, and she was wearing a dress that looked like a map of the world. In one hand she was holding a basketball, and the other hand was pulling a suitcase.

"Hello!" she said cheerfully. *"Bonjour! Hola! Guten Tag! Shalom!"* She said some other words I never heard before.

"All those words mean hello in other

languages," said Mr. Cooper. "I met Mrs. Barr when I was in Spain. She's visiting our country, and she agreed to come talk to you."

"Do you mind if I open a window?" asked Mrs. Barr. "It's a little stuffy in here."

"Go right ahead," said Mr. Cooper.

"Mr. Cooper tells me you're a real globe-trotter," Mr. Klutz said to Mrs. Barr.

"Is that why you have a basketball?" I asked.

"Not *that* kind of globetrotter, dumb-head!" whispered Andrea, rolling her eyes.*

"Oh, this isn't a basketball," Mrs. Barr told me. "It's a globe. Yes, I've been all over the world. I've visited a hundred and ninety-five countries."

"WOW," we all said, which is "MOM" upside down.

_____

* What are you looking down here for? The story is up THERE!

"Mrs. Barr has generously offered to spend this week at our school," said Mr. Klutz. "And she isn't charging us a penny. She's doing this out of the goodness of her heart. Isn't that *wonderful?*"

We gave her a round of applause. That's what you're supposed to do when people do nice things for free.

"I just *love* geography," said Mrs. Barr. "I am at your disposal."

"You're a garbage can?" I asked.

"Arlo!" shouted Andrea. "That's not nice!"

"Why do you have a suitcase?" Michael asked Mrs. Barr.

"I never know when I might want to

travel somewhere," she replied. "I like to be ready at all times. So I take it wherever I go."

"Do you take it when you go to the bathroom?" I asked.

"Yes!" she replied.

"How about in the shower?" asked Ryan. "Do you take your suitcase in the shower with you?"

"Well, no," she replied with a laugh. "I don't take it *in* the shower."

It would be weird to take a shower with a suitcase.

"Your necklaces are pretty!" said Andrea.

"Thank you!"

Andrea and Emily were oohing and

aahing over Mrs. Barr's jewelry.

"I got these necklaces on a trip to China," she said. "China is *amazing*. And I got this bracelet when I was visiting India. India is *amazing*. And I got these earrings in Brazil. Brazil is *amazing*!"

I still can't believe that people poke holes in their ears and stick stuff in them. I don't care what anybody says. That's just weird.

"Isn't travel amazing?" asked Mrs. Barr.

"Yes!" shouted all the girls.

"No!" shouted all the boys.

Mr. Cooper told us that Mrs. Barr speaks seven languages: English, Spanish, Turkish, Yiddish, Polish . . .

"Can you speak gibberish?" I asked.

"That's not a language, dumbhead!" said Andrea, rolling her eyes. I wish her eyes would roll right out of her head.

"Have you ever been to Egypt?" asked Neil.

"Oh yes!" Mrs. Barr replied. "I went inside the pyramids. It was *amazing*!"

Mrs. Barr thinks *every* place she goes is amazing. She probably thinks it's amazing when she goes to take out the garbage.

I don't get it. What's the big deal about going places? Why would you want to go someplace when you can stay home?

Going places is a drag. You have to go to the airport, take your shoes off, put your shoes on again, and sit around waiting for the plane to take off. Then you have to sit on the plane for a million hundred hours. Then, when you finally get to the place you're going, your parents drag you to a bunch of museums and other boring stuff.

Do you know what I think about as

soon as I get to the place I'm going? I think about when I can go home. I'd rather just stay home in the first place.

"I *love* traveling!" said Andrea, who loves everything I hate.

"Me too," said Emily, who agrees with everything Andrea says.

"Traveling allows you to experience other cultures," said Mr. Klutz.

"Other cultures are boring," I said.

"You get to try new foods," said Mr. Cooper.

"New foods are yucky," I said.

"Don't you want to become a well-rounded person, Arlo?" asked Andrea.

"I'd rather be a triangle," I told her.

"Well, by the end of the week," said Mrs. Barr, "I think you're going to change your mind. And you kids are going to learn *lots* about geography."

This was going to be the worst week in the history of weeks.

The Mystery of Mr. E

We were in Mr. Cooper's class that afternoon, working on a boring writing exercise.

"Pencils down," said Mr. Cooper. "It's time for fizz ed."

Yay! Fizz ed is my favorite subject. We walked a million hundred miles to the gym.

"Do you think we'll have relay races today?" Neil asked as we walked down the hall.

"Maybe we're going to climb the ropes," said Ryan.

Our fizz ed teacher is Miss Small. One time, she fell out of a tree and broke her leg.*

When we got to the gym, we saw the weirdest thing in the history of the world. There was a giant map that covered the whole floor! And the gym is *big*.

"What's up with the map?" I asked Miss Small.

---

* You can read about it in a book called *Miss Small Is off the Wall!*

"We have an exciting activity today," she replied.

And you'll never believe who walked into the door at that moment.

Nobody! It would hurt if you walked into a door. Didn't we go over that in chapter two?

But you'll never believe who walked into the door*way*. It was Mrs. Barr! She had her globe and suitcase with her.

"Do you mind if I open a window?" she asked.

"Go right ahead," said Miss Small.

"What's our activity?" asked Alexia.

"We're going on a globetrotting adventure," said Mrs. Barr.

"We're gonna play basketball?" I asked. "Cool!"

"Not *that* kind of globetrotting, dumbhead!" Andrea told me.

I was going to say something mean to Andrea, but I didn't have the chance because Mrs. Barr and Miss Small led us over to a part of the giant map. We were standing on the United States.

Mrs. Barr gathered everybody around her like a football team in a huddle. She lowered her voice as if she had a big secret.

"There's something fishy going on," she whispered.

Huh? Why is everybody always talking about fish?

"An international jewel thief named Mr. E is on the run," Mrs. Barr whispered. "We've got to catch him."

"How are we going to do that?" asked Emily.

"He left a series of clues that will tell us where he is," whispered Mrs. Barr. "Look!

There's the first clue!"

She went over and picked up a piece of yellow paper that was taped to the floor. She unfolded it and showed it to us . . .

I AM HIDING OUT NEAR A CLOCK
CALLED BIG BEN.
—Mr. E.

"Big Ben is in London!" shouted Alexia.

"That's right!" said Mrs. Barr. "Let's go to England!"

"We'll have to swim across the Atlantic Ocean," said Miss Small. "Everybody get down and swim!"

We all got down on the floor and

pretended to swim across the ocean. It's hard to swim without water. Mrs. Barr told us we swam over three thousand miles.

"Okay, we're in London, England," said Mrs. Barr. "And look! There's Big Ben."

"And there's another clue!" shouted Ryan.

Mrs. Barr picked up another piece of yellow paper. This is what it said . . .

I AM HIDING OUT IN THE SMALLEST
COUNTRY IN THE WORLD.
—Mr. E

"Rhode Island!" I shouted. "Mr. E is in Rhode Island!"

"Rhode Island isn't a country, Arlo," said Andrea, rolling her eyes.

"I knew that," I lied.

"The smallest country in the world is Vatican City!" shouted Andrea. "It's in the middle of Rome, Italy."

"That's right!" shouted Mrs. Barr.

Andrea smiled the smile she smiles to let everybody know she knows something nobody else knows.

"Let's go!" shouted Mrs. Barr. "Quickly! To Italy! Mr. E has stolen millions of dollars in jewelry. We've got to catch him!"

"Italy is *soooo* romantic," said Andrea. "Wouldn't you love to go to Italy, Arlo?"

"They have pizza there, right?" I asked.

"Yes, the best pizza in the world," said Andrea.

"I want to go there," I said. "Pizza is my favorite food."

"Ooooh," said Ryan. "A.J. and Andrea are talking about taking a trip to Italy together. They must be in *love*!"

"Maybe you two can go to Italy on your honeymoon," said Michael.

I was going to say something mean to the guys, but we all ran over to Italy on the map. It's shaped like a boot. Nobody knows why.

"Look!" shouted Mrs. Barr. "Here's another clue!"

I AM HIDING OUT IN A CONTINENT THAT
HAS MORE PEOPLE THAN ALL THE OTHER
CONTINENTS PUT TOGETHER.
—Mr. E

"I think it's Asia," said Ryan.

"That's right!" shouted Mrs. Barr. "Let's
go there!"

We all ran to Asia. It's really big, and it
has lots of countries in it.

"Look! Another clue!" shouted Mrs.
Barr.

I AM HIDING OUT ON A BOAT IN THE
LARGEST OCEAN IN THE WORLD.
—Mr. E

"The Pacific is the largest ocean!" Michael yelled.

"That's right!" shouted Mrs. Barr. "Let's go there!"

"This is good exercise!" said Miss Small. "Run!"

We all ran over to the Pacific Ocean. While we were running there, out of the corner of my eye I saw somebody going into the locker room at the other end of the gym.

"Who's that?" I asked.

"It could be Mr. E!" shouted Neil.

We all ran over to the locker room. Some guy was hiding behind the door. He was wearing a trench coat, a hat, and a pair of glasses with a fake nose under them.

"Freeze, dirtbag!" I shouted. "You're under arrest, Mr. E!"

"On what charge?" he asked, putting his hands in the air.

"Stealing millions of dollars' worth of jewels," Ryan said.

"I'm innocent!" shouted Mr. E. "I didn't steal a thing!"

Michael pulled off Mr. E's hat. Alexia pulled off his fake nose and glasses.

And you'll never believe in a million hundred years who Mr. E turned out to be.

I'm not going to tell you.

Okay, okay, I'll tell you.

It was Mrs. Roopy, our librarian!

"Gasp!" we all gasped.

"Mrs. Roopy!" I shouted. "*You're* Mr. E?"

"Roopy?" said Mrs. Roopy, running out the doorway. "Never heard of her."

That was weird.

"You kids did a great job finding Mr. E," said Mrs. Barr. "See? You know more about geography than you think."

We walked a million hundred miles back to our classroom.

"Bummer in the summer," I said as we walked down the hall. "I thought Mr. E was going to be a *real* international jewel thief. He turned out to be Mrs. Roopy in one of her disguises."

"It was just a scavenger hunt, Arlo!" said Andrea. "Mrs. Barr made up all those clues as a way to teach us geography."

"I knew that," I lied.

I hate when grown-ups sneak in learning while we're trying to have fun. They think we won't notice. I can't believe I fell for it.

It's not fair!

Less Is More

I could hardly sleep that night. I kept thinking about how Mrs. Barr tricked us into learning geography. That makes me so mad! No way I'm gonna fall for that again.

The next day, Mr. Cooper didn't even *try* to teach us math. As soon as he saw

Mrs. Barr come into the class with her suitcase, he closed his eyes and rubbed his forehead.

He sure rubs his forehead a lot. I guess he needs to moisturize.

"Konnichiwa!" Mrs. Barr said as she went over and opened the window. "That means hello in Japanese."

"Have you visited Japan?" asked Andrea.

"I've been there many times," Mrs. Barr replied. "Japan is *amazing*!"

"How about the United States?" asked Ryan. "Have you traveled around *our* country?"

"Sure!" she replied. "I've been all over America. It is *amazing*!"

"Did you go to the Grand Canyon?" asked Emily.

"No," replied Mrs. Barr.

"How about Mount Rushmore?" asked Alexia.

"Nope. But I went to the SPAM Museum in Minnesota."

WHAT?!

"There's a museum about SPAM?" Ryan asked.

"Oh yes!" said Mrs. Barr. "It is *amazing*! Did you know that SPAM stands for spiced ham?* I also visited the largest ball of twine in the world. It's in Kansas and it's over ten feet tall! It is *amazing*!"

---

* I thought it stood for "Something Posing as Meat."

Wait. Mrs. Barr has never been to the Grand Canyon or Mount Rushmore, but she's visited the SPAM Museum and a giant ball of twine? That lady is weird.

"Let's talk about geography!" said Mrs. Barr.

"I know something about geography,"

said Little Miss Know-It-All. "The word 'geography' comes from ancient Greece. It means to write or describe the earth."

"I didn't know that!" said Mrs. Barr.

Andrea smiled the smile that she smiles to let everybody know she knows something nobody else knows.

"Let's talk about water," said Mrs. Barr. "Did you know that water covers more than two-thirds of the earth *blah blah blah blah*...*"

She went on about water for a million hundred minutes. I was starting to feel sleepy again.

"... *blah blah blah blah* the Nile is the longest river in the world *blah blah blah*

blah over four thousand miles long and *blah blah blah blah* . . ."

I felt like my eyelids had ten-pound weights on them.

". . . *blah blah blah blah* Antarctica is the coldest continent *blah blah blah blah.* It's the only continent that gets larger and smaller as it freezes and melts and *blah blah blah blah* . . . Antarctica . . . Antarctica . . . Antarctica . . . Antarctica . . . Antarctica . . . Antarctica . . . Antarctica . . ."

The next thing I knew, I was having a wild dream. . . .

I'm in Antarctica. There are no schools here. Nobody has to learn stuff. Nobody has to wear a tie or go to tea parties. There are no bedtimes, and no Andrea. Nobody is making fun of me.

I don't have to do anything I don't want to do in Antarctica. I'm eating frozen pizza, because all the pizza is frozen here. I'm running around and playing freeze tag, because that's the only kind of tag you can play in Antarctica. My friends are a family of penguins. Tag! You're it!

There are lots of water slides and theme parks and candy stores here. You don't have to buy anything. Everything is free. All the toilet bowls are upside down in Antarc—

"Wake up, A.J.," said Mr. Cooper.

"Huh? What?"

I picked my head up off my desk. Mrs. Barr was gone. So were all the kids.

"Where is everybody?" I asked.

"They went to the art room," Mr. Cooper told me. "You were sleeping so peacefully, I didn't want to wake you."

Mr. Cooper and I went to the art room. Our art teacher, Ms. Hannah, was in there with Mrs. Barr and all the kids. They were sitting at a big table and there were feathers, beads, glue, and other art stuff scattered around.

"Did you have a nice nap, Arlo?" asked Andrea.

I ignored her.

"What are you guys doing?" I asked.

"We're making masks!" said Ms. Hannah.

"Different cultures in countries all over the world have worn masks," said Mrs. Barr. "For example, in China, Africa, Austria, Mexico, Brazil . . ."

Uh-oh. She was trying to teach us about geography again.

"Masks have been used as disguises, or for protection, entertainment, or in religious ceremonies," said Mrs. Barr.

I wasn't paying attention.

"The oldest mask in the world dates back to 8300 BCE," said Mrs. Barr.

I couldn't take it anymore.

"I'm not going to learn *anything* about masks!" I announced. "I'm not falling for *that* old trick again."

"You don't have to learn anything," Ms. Hannah told me. "You can just make a mask for the fun of it."

"I'm making a carnival mask," said Alexia.

"I'm making a surgical mask," said Neil.

"I'm making a hockey mask," said Michael.

"You can make any kind of mask you'd like," said Ms. Hannah. "Be creative. Use your imaginations!"

"The student who makes my favorite mask wins a prize," said Mrs. Barr.

"Oooooh, I *love* prizes!" said Andrea.

"What's the prize?" asked Ryan.

"The prize is that I will wear your mask for the rest of the week," said Mrs. Barr.

That's a weird prize. But everybody was hard at work on their masks.

I didn't know what kind of mask to make. Maybe I was still groggy from my nap. The other kids were almost finished. I didn't want to make a dumb mask.

"Five more minutes," announced Ms. Hannah. "Then it's clean-up time."

Finally, the time was up. All I had was a plain black cloth.

"*That's* your mask, dude?" asked Michael. "You didn't put anything on it."

"A.J., your mask is lame," said Neil.

All the kids were laughing, like my mask was the funniest thing in the history of the world.

"Well, I happen to *like* A.J.'s mask," said Ms. Hannah. "It's simple. Sometimes in art, less is more."

"I think A.J.'s mask is cool," said Mrs. Barr. "You win the prize, A.J. May I wear your mask for the rest of the week?"

"Sure!" I said.

Everybody stopped laughing.

Ha! In their face! I made the best mask. So nah-nah-nah boo-boo on everybody.

International Day

"Happy International Day!" Mrs. Barr said when I came to class the next morning. She was wearing the mask I made.

"What's International Day?" I asked.

"Each of you is going to choose a country," said Mrs. Barr. "Any country in the world. You'll spend the morning learning about your country online. Then you'll give a short presentation to the class, as if you were the leader of that country. Doesn't that sound like fun?"

"Yes!" said all the girls.

"No!" said all the boys.

"I think it's a *great* idea!" said Mr. Cooper. "The kids will learn a lot, plus they can practice their research and public-speaking skills."

It sounded like a *horrible* idea to me. Learning? Research? Public speaking? I thought I was gonna die.

Andrea was so excited, she could barely stay in her seat.

"My country is going to be—"

But Andrea didn't have the chance to finish her sentence.

"Shhhhhh!" said Mrs. Barr. "Don't tell us the name of your country until it's time for your presentation. Let's make it a surprise."

"I love surprises!" said Andrea.

"Me too!" said Emily.

We walked a million hundred miles to the computer lab, where there was a computer set up for each of us. Mrs. Barr passed out pads and pencils so we could take notes about our country. Andrea got permission to use her smartphone, because she has to be a big show-off all the time.

"What should we look up?" asked Ryan.

"Search for interesting facts about your country," said Mrs. Barr. "Where is it located? What do the people wear? What do they eat? What language to they speak? Things like that."

Everybody started looking stuff up. Well, everybody but me. I couldn't think of a country I wanted to learn about. Ryan was sitting next to me. I leaned over to see what country he chose.

"No peeking at other people's computers," said Mrs. Barr. "We want it to be a surprise when you give your presentation."

I was bored. I looked up a bunch of stuff about football. Did you know that a guy with only half a foot once kicked a sixty-three-yard field goal? It's true! Go ahead, look it up if you don't believe me.

"Isn't this *wonderful*?" Mrs. Barr said as we were all looking up stuff. "Maybe someday all the nations of the world will work together like this so people can live in peace and harmony."

Everybody worked hard all the way to lunchtime. Well, everybody except me. But I learned a lot about football.

After lunch, we went back to Mr. Cooper's class.

"Okay, who wants to give the first

International Day presentation?" asked Mrs. Barr.

"I do!" shouted Andrea, of course.

"Go ahead, Andrea."

Andrea rushed up to the front of the room with her notes. She couldn't wait to show how smart she was.

"I am the queen of Norway," Andrea said. "My country is in northern Europe. It's a little bigger than New Mexico. We are one of the largest seafood producers in the world."

Why is everybody always talking about fish?

"More than five million people live in my country," Andrea continued. "We speak Norwegian and we have twenty-nine letters in our alphabet. Our capital city is Oslo. Our national animal is the moose, and *blah blah blah blah . . ."*

What a snoozefest. They shouldn't call that country Norway. They should call it Boreway! Andrea went on for a million hundred minutes. I wasn't really listening. I just wanted Andrea to keep talking until dismissal so I wouldn't have to give a presentation.

"... and *that's* why we eat reindeer meatballs in Norway."

"Very good, Andrea!" said Mr. Cooper. "You certainly taught us a lot about Norway. Who wants to go next?"

We all stared at the floor.

"How about you, A.J.?" said Mr. Cooper.

Oh no. Not *me*.

"A.J.! A.J.! A.J.!" everybody chanted.

I didn't know what to say. I didn't know what to do. I had to think fast.

"You *did* do research on a country, didn't you?" asked Mrs. Barr.

"Sure I did," I lied.

I went up to the front of the room. Everybody was staring at me. It was the worst moment of my life.

"Don't you have any notes, A.J.?" asked Mrs. Barr.

"No, I, uh . . . memorized everything."

"Impressive!" said Mr. Cooper. "Please

begin, A.J."

"I am the president of . . . Flurgenstan," I said. It was the first thing I could think of.

"Hmmm, I've never heard of Flurgenstan," said Mrs. Barr. "And I've been all over the world."

"We are a brand-new country," I explained. "We just started last week."

"Go on, Mr. President," said Mr. Cooper.

"Flurgenstan is a beautiful country," I said, "with lots of trees and animals and, uh . . . food."

I made up a bunch of stuff about Flurgenstan. I told everybody the national bird is the hummingbird. The national food is chicken tacos. They have a lot of kangaroos and yaks. I just said whatever popped into my mind.

"There are no nerds in Flurgenstan," I said, looking at Andrea. "And you know how skate parks usually close at sundown? Well, in Flurgenstan they stay open all night."

"Fascinating!" said Mrs. Barr.

"Would you like to see the Flurgenstan national dance?" I asked.

"Yeah!" everybody shouted.

I made up a totally dumb dance, jumping around and waving my arms in the air.

Everybody was nodding their heads.* It looked like they were actually buying it! Well, everybody except Andrea.

"Are we allowed to ask questions?" she said.

"Certainly!" said Mrs. Barr. "That's how we learn."

"Where is Flurgenstan located, Mr.

_____

* What a bunch of dumbheads!

President? Hmmmm?" Andrea asked. Then she smiled the smile she smiles when she knows somebody doesn't know something.

"Flurgenstan," I said, "is a small island off the coast of . . . Maratooga."

I made that up too.

"Oh, yeah?" asked Andrea. "And what language do you speak in Flurgenstan?"

"It's a very beautiful language," I told her. "We speak Flurgenstanian."

"Uh-huh," said Andrea. "Is there a Flurgenstan national anthem?"

"Uh, yeah."

"Would you be able to sing the Flurgenstan national anthem for us?" asked Mrs. Barr.

"Oh gee, I don't know . . ." I said.

"Come on, Arlo!" said Andrea. "Sing the Flurgenstan national anthem for us."

"SING IT! SING IT! SING IT!" everybody chanted.

I didn't know what to say. I didn't know what to do. I had to think fast. So I sang the first thing that came into my mind. . . .

Oh give me a home
Where the kangaroos roam,
and the yak and the hummingbirds play.
Where seldom is heard
from a dweeb or a nerd,
And the skate parks stay open all day.
Home, home on Flurgenstan—

"That sounds a lot like 'Home on the Range,'" said Mr. Cooper.

"Yeah," I told him. "Flurgenstan is such a new country, we haven't had time to write our national anthem yet."

Andrea looked like she was about to explode.

"There's no country called Flurgenstan!" she yelled. "I just looked it up on my smartphone. Arlo is making all this stuff up!"

"I am not!" I yelled.

"Are too!"

"R2D2!"

We went on like that for a while.

"Oh, yeah?" I finally said. "Well, as the president of Flurgenstan, I declare war on Norway!"

"As the queen of Norway," Andrea said, "I declare war on Flurgenstan!"

"I'm on Norway's side!" shouted Emily.

"I'm on Flurgenstan's side!" shouted Alexia.

And that's how World War III began.

The Truth about Mrs. Barr

After school, the gang and I decided to hang around the playground for a while before going home. Andrea and Emily came over to bother us, of course. They couldn't stop talking about Mrs. Barr.

"Mrs. Barr is so cool," said Andrea. "She's traveled all over the world."

"When I grow up, I want to be a globe-trotter like her," said Emily.

"No way," I told her. "You don't even *play* basketball."

"Very funny, Arlo," said Andrea.*

"It must be nice to have a job where you get to travel all the time," said Ryan.

"That's not a job," I said. "Mrs. Barr isn't getting paid. If you don't get paid, it's not a job."

"Then how does she earn a living?" asked Michael.

"Beats me," said Neil.

"I'm sad that tomorrow is Mrs. Barr's

---

*I don't care. I'm going to keep using that joke until somebody laughs at it.

last day at our school," said Andrea.

"Not *me*," I said.

"What do you have against Mrs. Barr?" asked Neil.

"Yeah," said Alexia. "She's a nice lady."

I had given this a lot of thought. Ever since Mrs. Barr walked into our classroom, there was something about

her that bothered me.

"That lady is no geography teacher," I announced. "She didn't even know what the word 'geography' *meant* until Andrea told her."

"She never *said* she was a geography teacher, Arlo," said Andrea. "She's just somebody who Mr. Cooper met on his trip to Spain."

"That's right," I agreed. "She's just a *stranger.* I'll tell you what I think. Mrs. Barr is a phony. She's probably a *criminal.*"

"WHAT?!" everybody said.

"Are you crazy, A.J.?" asked Ryan.

"Look," I explained. "Do you know why Mrs. Barr travels all over the world? It's because she's on the run from the cops! She's probably a jewel thief."

"That's just nuts, A.J.," said Michael.

"Oh, yeah?" I said. "What about all that jewelry she wears? I bet it's stolen. That's why she doesn't have a job. She probably stashes her stolen jewels in that suitcase she rolls around all the time."

"Arlo, are you feeling okay?" asked Andrea. "Maybe you need to talk to Dr. Brad."

Dr. Brad is our school counselor. Kids can talk to him if they have problems. But I didn't have any problems.

"Think about it," I said. "Mrs. Barr loves wearing masks. You know who else wears masks?"

"Who?" everybody asked.

"Robbers!" I said. "People who steal stuff."

"That's ridiculous, Arlo!" said Andrea. "Mrs. Barr is a world traveler. She's trying to help us learn geography. She's not even getting paid. She's teaching us out of the goodness of her heart. You should be thanking her instead of calling her a criminal."

"Yeah, well, I don't trust her."

"Dude, every time a new grown-up comes to our school, you say you don't trust them," said Ryan. "You say they're an imposter."

"Sometimes people are who they say they are, A.J.," said Alexia.

"Yeah," said Neil. "Sometimes people do nice things just because they're nice people."

"Hey, you don't have to believe me," I told them.

"Good, because I don't," said Ryan.

Even my best friends were ganging up on me. I went home by myself.

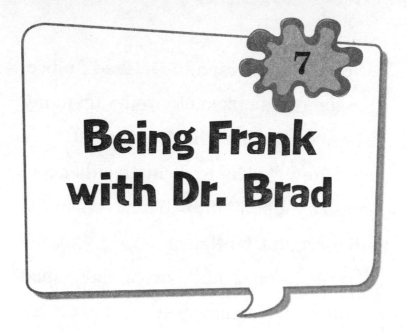

Being Frank
with Dr. Brad

The next day was Friday. After we pledged the allegiance, Mr. Cooper told us to turn to page twenty-three in our math books. That's when an announcement came over the loudspeaker.

"Mr. Cooper, please send A.J. to Dr. Brad's office."

"Ooooooooh!" everybody ooooooohed.

I didn't want to go to Dr. Brad's office. One time, he hooked electrodes up to my head and gave me a lie detector test.

But I didn't want to do math either. So I walked a million hundred miles down the hall to Dr. Brad's office.

Dr. Brad looks like one of those mad scientists in the movies who strap people to a dentist chair and torture them. He said I should lie down on his couch.

He took out a big magnifying glass and looked in my eyes. Then he looked in my ears. Then he looked in my mouth. Then he looked up my nose.*

"Velly interesting," he said. Dr. Brad

---

* Are you enjoying the story so far? Can I get you a cookie?

talks funny. "Eez anyzing bozering you, A.J.?"

"No," I replied. "I'm fine."

"Any problems you vant to tell me?"

"No."

"A.J.," Dr. Brad said, "may I be frank viz you?"

"Sure," I told him. "I don't care what you call yourself."

"Do you know vut zuh vord 'paranoid' means, A.J.?"

"Yeah," I said. "That's what you wear when you jump out of an airplane."

"Ha-ha-ha," laughed Dr. Brad. "Most amusing. Zat eez a para*chute*."

"Oh," I said. "Paranoid is somebody who rides in an ambulance."

"No, zat eez a para*medic*."

"I know," I said. "Isn't a paranoid one of those bugs that lives inside your body?"

"Zat eez a para*site*," said Dr. Brad. "Zuh vord 'paranoid' means ven you are alvays suspicious and don't trust anyvun."

"Oh," I said, "that was my next guess."

"A.J., I'm going to be frank," said Dr. Brad.

"Okay," I said. "I'll be A.J."

"I hear zat you have been telling zee

ozzer keeds zat Mrs. Barr eez zum kind of criminal."

"Yeah, I think she's an international jewel thief."

"A.J., let me be frank," said Dr. Brad.

"I already said you could be Frank," I told him.

"Mrs. Barr eez a velly nice voomahn," said Dr. Brad. "Eet eez zo kind of her to geeve her time to teach you keeds about geography."

"Then why does she open the window every time she walks into a room?" I asked. "Maybe she wants to be able to escape in case the cops show up."

Dr. Brad took off his glasses and rubbed his forehead.

"A.J., let's be frank," he said.

"Both of us?" I asked. "Won't that be confusing?"

"Vut eef Mrs. Barr zimply vants zum fresh air? Maybe zat's vy she opens zuh vindow."

"Or maybe she's a robber," I said.

Dr. Brad took off his glasses again and rubbed his forehead some more. I guess he needs to moisturize, like Mr. Cooper.

"Go back to zuh classroom, A.J."

"Okay, Frank," I said.

"My name eez not Frank!" he shouted.

Sheesh, what is his problem? *He's* the one who told me to call him Frank.

What's in Mrs. Barr's Suitcase?

When I left Dr. Brad's office, I went to the vomitorium, where everybody was eating lunch. We all had peanut butter and jelly sandwiches, because that's the law.

"What did Dr. Brad say to you?" asked Ryan.

"Nothing," I replied. "He just wanted to tell me that his name is Frank."

"So I guess you still think Mrs. Barr is a jewel thief?" asked Alexia.

"Sure I do," I said. "I can prove it to you."

"How?" everybody asked.

"All we need to do is look inside that suitcase she pulls around," I said. "Come on, follow me."

We cleaned off our plates and left the vomitorium. I didn't know where Mrs. Barr was, but she had to be around the school somewhere. We just had to find her.

"Shhhhhh!" I said as we sneaked down the hallway.

We sneaked around like secret agents, peeking into classrooms. It was cool. I love sneaking around pretending to be a spy.

"What are we gonna do when we find her?" asked Neil.

"One of us needs to distract her," I told him, "while the others open her suitcase and see what's inside."

"I think that's an invasion of privacy," whispered Andrea.

"Your *face* is an invasion of privacy!" I whispered back.

We sneaked around for a million hundred minutes. No sign of Mrs. Barr.

"This is silly, Arlo," said Andrea. "She probably went out for lunch."

"She's hiding," I said, sneaking around a corner. "She must know we're after her."

That's when the weirdest thing in the history of the world happened. We came to a door.

Well, that's not the weird part. We come to doors all the time. The weird part was what happened next.

The door was to a broom closet where our custodian, Miss Lazar, keeps cleaning supplies and stuff. There was a noise on the other side of the door. It sounded like snoring.

"Shhhhhh!" I *shhhhh*-ed. "What's that?"

"I didn't hear anything," said Michael.

I put my hand on the doorknob. I was afraid to open it because in scary movies every time somebody opens a door a monster jumps out. But I gathered up my courage and pulled open the door.

And you'll never believe in a million hundred years what we found in the closet.

I'm not going to tell you.

Okay, okay, I'll tell you.

It was Mrs. Barr! And she was lying on a cot, sleeping!

"This is our chance!" I whispered. "Let's see what's inside her suitcase. I bet it's filled with diamonds and rubies and stuff."

We got down on our hands and knees. The suitcase had a bunch of zippers on it.

"Hurry up!" Michael whispered. "She could wake up any second!"

"Shhhhhh!" I *shhhhh*-ed.

Finally, I found the right zipper. I started pulling it.

"Hey!"

Mrs. Barr jumped up from the cot.

"What are you kids doing in here?" she asked.

"*I'll* ask the questions," I said. "What are *you* doing in here?"

"Taking a nap!" replied Mrs. Barr. "I'm still a little jet-lagged. What are you doing with my suitcase?"

"We want to know what you have in there," I said.

"Well, I'll *show* you what I have in there," Mrs. Barr replied as she pulled the zipper. "It's underwear! See?"*

She pulled out a pair of underwear. It had a picture of the Eiffel Tower on it. Then she took out another pair of under-wear that said "I LOVE ITALY" on it. Then she took out *another* pair of underwear that had a map of Australia on it.

---

*It should be a law that every book has to have a scene with underwear in it.

"Wow," I said. "You have a lot of underwear!"

"It's not mine. It's for my dog," said Mrs. Barr. "My hobby is collecting doggie underwear from around the world."

Doggie underwear? That's a weird thing

to collect. But I guess it's not illegal. Mrs. Barr closed her suitcase.

"We're sorry," said Andrea. "We didn't mean to disturb your nap."

"No worries," Mrs. Barr replied.

We left the closet and went to class.

"See, I *told* you, Arlo!" said Andrea. "Mrs. Barr isn't a criminal."

Bummer in the summer! I hate it when Andrea is right. Why can't a suitcase full of doggie underwear fall on her head?

The Big Surprise Ending

It was almost time for my favorite part of the day—dismissal! Everybody was gathering up their pencil cases and backpacks. That's when Mrs. Barr came into our classroom. She was wearing the mask I made in art class.

"I just wanted to say goodbye," she said.

"We're going to miss you," everybody

said. Some of the kids went over to give Mrs. Barr hugs.

"I'm going to miss you too," she said as she went over and opened the window.

"Where are you going to travel next?" asked Ryan.

"Oh, I don't know," Mrs. Barr replied. "Maybe Istanbul. That's in Turkey. Istanbul is the only major city that is in *two* continents. You can actually stand with one foot in Asia and one foot in Europe."

"Cool!" everybody said.

"Or maybe I'll go to Indonesia," said Mrs. Barr. "Did you know that Indonesia has more than thirteen thousand islands?"*

---

* That must be where Thousand Island dressing comes from.

Brrrrrriiiiiiinnnnngggg!

The dismissal bell rang. That's when the weirdest thing in the history of the world happened. Mr. Klutz came into our classroom.

Well, that's not the weird part. Mr. Klutz comes into our classroom all the time. The weird part was what happened next.

"This has been a wonderful week, Mrs. Barr," said Mr. Klutz. "I wanted to thank you for giving up your valuable time and teaching our students about geography."

"I have had a *lovely* week," said Mrs. Barr. "Thank *you* for letting me visit your school."

And you'll never believe who burst through the door at that moment.

Nobody! You can't burst through a door! When are you going to learn?

But you'll never believe who burst through the door*way*.

It was four policemen!

"Freeze, dirtbag!" one of them shouted. "You're under arrest!"

"*Who's* under arrest?" we all shouted.

The police officers pointed at Mrs. Barr.

"Gasp!" everybody gasped.

"What did Mrs. Barr do?" asked Mr. Klutz.

"She is the notorious Globetrotting Jewel Thief," said one of the officers.

"I *knew* it!" I shouted.

"Oh, she's a clever one," the officer continued. "We've chased her from England to Italy to Asia, and across the Pacific Ocean. She hides out in schools wherever she goes. Every time we're about to catch her, she slips away. But now we've finally nabbed her."

"Mrs. Barr, you've gone too far," one of the other cops said.

"There must be some mistake," Mr. Cooper said. "Mrs. Barr is just a nice lady I met on vacation."

"Oh yeah?" said one of the officers as he

grabbed Mrs. Barr's suitcase. "Let's have a look in here."

"She keeps her doggie underwear collection in there!" Andrea shouted.

"*Sure* she does," the officer said as he opened the suitcase and picked up some doggie underwear. "But underneath, the suitcase is filled with stolen jewels! See?"

He held up a fistful of necklaces and bracelets.

"Gasp!" everybody gasped.

"I told you!" I shouted. "*Nobody* needs a whole suitcase to carry their doggie underwear!"

"What do you have to say for yourself, Mrs. Barr?" asked Mr. Klutz.

"But . . . but . . ." she stuttered.

We all giggled because Mrs. Barr said "but," which sounds just like "butt" even though it only has one *T*.

"You like taking trips, lady?" one of the officers asked. "Well, you're going to take *another* trip . . . to *jail*!"

"How interesting," said one of the other officers. "Her name is Barr, and that's what she's going to be behind. Bars!"

"Not if *I* can help it!" shouted Mrs. Barr.

And you'll never believe what happened next.

"You'll never catch me, coppers!" Mrs. Barr yelled as she grabbed her suitcase. Then she ran over to the open window and jumped out of it!

"Gasp!" we all gasped.

"Get her!" shouted the cops.

They all jumped out the window and chased Mrs. Barr into the street.

"Sayonara," she hollered as she ran away. *"Au revoir! Arrivederci! Auf Wiedersehen! Adios, amigos!"*

Nobody said anything for a long time. It was Mr. Cooper who broke the silence.

"I feel terrible," he said. "I had no idea that Mrs. Barr was a thief. She seemed like such a nice lady."

"That's okay, Mr. Cooper," said Mr. Klutz.

"Nobody could have guessed that Mrs. Barr was a criminal," said Andrea.

"Hey, *I* guessed she was a criminal!" I shouted at Andrea. "I tried to tell you, but you thought I was crazy!"

"A.J. was right all along," said Michael.

"Now we know why Mrs. Barr had that

suitcase with her all the time," said Alexia.

"And now we know why she opened the window every time she came into a room," said Neil. "So she could jump out of it if the police showed up."

"It seems so obvious now," said Ryan. "But except for A.J., we fell for it hook, line, and sinker."

WHY IS EVERYBODY ALWAYS TALKING ABOUT FISH?

Andrea had on her mean face. I knew why she was mad—because I was right and she was wrong.

"This was all *your* fault, Arlo!" she said.

"What?!"

"If you had been able to find Spain on

the map," said Andrea, "Mrs. Barr would have never come to our school in the first place!"

"*My* fault?" I shouted. "*You* believed everything Mrs. Barr said! I'm the only one who knew she was a thief!"

"Ooooh," said Ryan. "A.J. and Andrea are having a spat. They must be in *love*!"

"When are you gonna get married?" asked Michael.

If those guys weren't my best friends, I would hate them.

Well, that's pretty much what happened. Maybe Mr. Cooper will stop showing us boring pictures from his vacations. Maybe the Great Lakes will stop bragging about how great they are. Maybe Dr. Brad will stop calling himself Frank. Maybe grown-ups will put on moisturizer so they don't have to rub their foreheads so much. Maybe everybody will stop talking about fish for no reason. Maybe the police will finally catch Mrs. Barr and put her in jail. Maybe dogs will stop wearing underwear.

But it won't be easy!

More weird books from Dan Gutman

My Weird School

My Weird School Graphic Novels

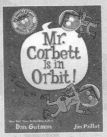

My Weirder School

My Weirdest School

My Weirder-est School

My Weird School Fast Facts

My Weird School Daze

My Weird Tips